CHILDREN
OF THE
GREAT LAKE

PERCY TREZISE

Angus&Robertson
An imprint of HarperCollins*Publishers*

AN ANGUS & ROBERTSON BOOK
An imprint of HarperCollinsPublishers

First published in Australia in 1992 by
CollinsAngus&Robertson Publishers Pty Limited (ACN 009 913 517)
A division of HarperCollinsPublishers (Australia) Pty Limited
25 Ryde Road, Pymble NSW 2073, Australia

HarperCollinsPublishers (New Zealand) Limited
31 View Road, Glenfield, Auckland 10, New Zealand

HarperCollinsPublishers Limited
77– 85 Fulham Palace Road, London W6 8JB, United Kingdom

National Library of Australia
Cataloguing-in-Publication data:

Trezise, Percy.
    Children of the great lake.
    ISBN 0 207 17677 9.
    1. Aborigines, Australian—Legends—Juvenile literature.
    I. Title.
398.20994

Printed in the People's Republic of China.

5 4 3 2 1
95 94 93 92

Foreword

A group of scientists led by Dr. Tom Torgersen investigated the Gulf of Carpentaria and discovered that during the Ice Age, the Gulf had dried up, forming a land bridge between Australia and New Guinea. The bridge was called Sahul Land.

They estimated that about 36,000 years ago, a freshwater lake began to fill in Sahul Land, and by 26,000 years ago, it was one of the largest freshwater lakes in the world.

The lake is remembered in Aboriginal oral history. There are many legends which describe the huge shallow lake, its swamps and islands teeming with aquatic life, and the people and events which shaped the course of their lives.

Rising sea levels at the end of the Ice Age, about 10,000 years ago, gradually drowned the lake with salt water, and it became the Gulf of Carpentaria.

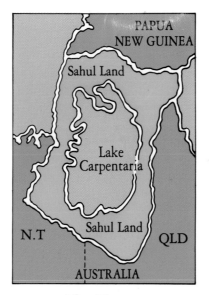

After Torgersen

The Bird people lived along the shore of the great lake. Each clan had its own Bird Dreaming. Ngali, and his sister Mayli, were of the Brolga Dreaming. Their clan country lay between two rivers which flowed into the lake.

The people used canoes and rafts to hunt and fish on the lake. They lived in small villages scattered among big paperbark trees growing everywhere along the fringes of the lake and rivers.

During the warm rainy season the people moved up-river to drier country to hunt large animals. Their forest country was full of kangaroos, kadimakaras, emus and other types of animals. At dawn the hunters would go out and quietly encircle a herd of kadimakara, selecting a young male as their quarry.

When the hunters were close, they would yell to stampede the
kadimakara and the chosen animal would became the target of
the spear-men. It would soon be crippled by spears and dispatched
swiftly with a heavy stone hatchet. The animal would then be cut
up, the meat bundled in paperbark and carried back to camp.

During the cool dry season the Bird people spent most of their time harvesting food around the lake's edge, which abounded with geese, ducks, brolgas and other water fowl. There were many kinds of fish, and a large freshwater turtle was a favourite food.

Ngali and Mayli liked to play with their cousins, Jadianta and Gulna. Their fathers had made them a walpa and they paddled it about in shallow water to gather waterlily roots, to spear fish and to trap big red-clawed crayfish in woven pots.

One evening they were fishing off the outer reed beds when a strong
east wind came up suddenly and blew the walpa away from shore.
Jadianta threw the anchor rock and line overboard, but the rope
broke and they drifted out into the great lake.

Away from shore, the water was rougher and the children were forced to lie on the walpa and hang on as they could not paddle against the fierce wind. They were scared as they knew that of all the people blown out into the lake on walpas, none had ever returned. Only a rising full moon watched them going.

Days later they woke at dawn to see they were drifting to a small island. It was covered with trees but there were no gunyahs, canoes or people. Only small flocks of curious birds watched their arrival.

The children were cold and hungry and after pulling the walpa ashore, they looked about for something to eat. They had lost their fishing gear and paddles. Gulna said, 'There's some firestick wood over there. You boys make a fire while we find some food to cook.'

The children worked hard. In a few days they had built a gunyah and had made string for fishing lines and throwing sticks to get birds. Although they now had food and shelter, they were worried about getting back home.

Ngali said, 'Our home is under the rising sun. The wind always comes from that direction in the dry season, and we can't paddle the walpa against it like we could a canoe. We will have to stay here until the monsoon winds come in six moon's time, to blow us back home again.'

The boys were out hunting one day when they made a terrifying discovery — they were sharing the island with a Wonambi, a huge monster snake. It was swallowing a large bird. Ngali and Jadianta were scared as they knew the monster snake also ate people.

As they ran away Jadianta said, 'We will have to leave the island before it gets hungry again. When it wakes up in a few days it will come looking for us. It's too big for us to kill.'

The children decided to make four new paddles for the walpa so they could escape the island as soon as possible. They found some pieces of driftwood and shaped it into paddles by charring the wood in the fire and scraping it back. The boys also found another anchor rock and made a rope for it.

They gathered long poles of wood and kept one burning in the
fire all the time so they could fight the Wonambi off with fire if
it came back. The girls had to find and cook as much food as they
could to take with them when they left the island.

Gulna and Mayli were out hunting when they saw the dreaded
Wonambi. It was hiding in the reeds trying to catch a jabiru.

The monster snake was hungry and hunting again. Gulna and
Mayli ran to warn the boys. It was time to leave the island.

The girls were running through long grass behind the beach when
they found a bark canoe. They thought it could have been blown
up in a storm. It looked good and strong and they knew it could
take them back home. They ran to camp with the good news.

The boys looked over the canoe and said the sewn ends would
need resealing with a heated gum and wax mixture. Together
the children carried the canoe back to camp to start work on it.
They hoped to finish it before dark and get away from the island.

The boys got gum by heating the trunk of a grasstree in the fire.
Gulna still had some knobs of beeswax in her hair put there by
her mother while getting honey, so they heated this and mixed
it with the gum to seal the ends of the canoe.

The girls kept watch for the Wonambi while cooking and wrapping food to take with them. It was nearly dark when they loaded the canoe and paddled away towards the rising moon and home.

Happiness at the thought of heading home, and that they had escaped the hungry Wonambi, kept them paddling steadily down the silver moon-track. When they were well away from the island, Ngali told Mayli and Gulna to rest and have a sleep.

He and Jadianta paddled on under a waxing moon. When they bumped into a mudbank with reeds on it they threw the anchor out and lay back to sleep.

They were wakened at dawn by the calls of birds all about them. There were flamingoes, jabirus, geese, ducks, pelicans and their own special Dreaming bird, the graceful brolgas. They knew the birds meant the coast was not far off.

They ate some of their food and drank some water, then paddled through the reed-banks and headed for the sunrise. The lake was silver and calm, and although there was no land in sight, they knew they would reach the shore sometime that day.

In the middle of the afternoon trees on the shoreline rose to view, and later, when they saw the river-mouth, the children cheered. They needed only a slight alteration to be heading straight for home. A rising, near-full moon over the village showed they had been gone a full moon cycle.

The children paddled round a reed-bed and yelled to people in the village, who looked towards them in disbelief. Then a great shout went up and they saw their parents and all the other people running to the shore, laughing and crying, and wading out to meet the children they had thought were lost forever.